PUFFIN BOOKS

THE GREAT SLOTH RACE

Dick King-Smith served in the Grenadier Guards during the Second World War, and afterwards spent twenty years as a farmer in Gloucestershire, the county of his birth. Many of his stories are inspired by his farming experiences. Later he taught at a village primary school. His first book, *The Fox Busters*, was published in 1978. Since then he has written a great number of children's books, including *The Sheep-Pig* (winner of the *Guardian* Award and filmed as *Babe*), *Harry's Mad*, *Noah's Brother*, *The Hodgeheg*, *Martin's Mice*, *Ace*, *The Cuckoo Child* and *Harriet's Hare* (winner of the Children's Book Award in 1995). At the British Book Awards in 1991 he was voted Children's Author of the Year. He has three children and twelve grandchildren and two great-grandchildren, and lives now in a seventeenth-century cottage a crow's-flight from the house where he was born.

Some other books by Dick King-Smith

BLESSU

CLEVER DUCK

DUMPLING

GEORGE SPEAKS

THE HODGEHEG

A HODGEHEG STORY:
KING MAX THE LAST

THE INVISIBLE DOG

A NARROW SQUEAK AND
OTHER ANIMAL STORIES

PHILIBERT THE FIRST AND
OTHER STORIES

POPPET

SMASHER

THE SWOOSE

Monsignor A.J. Hetherington School

Dick King-Smith

The Great Sloth Race

Illustrated by Tim Warnes

PUFFIN BOOKS

For nimble Peter – T.W.

PUFFIN BOOKS

Penguin Books Ltd, 27 Wrights Lane, London W8 5TZ, England
Penguin Putnam Inc., 375 Hudson Street, New York, New York 10014, USA
Penguin Books Australia Ltd, Ringwood, Victoria, Australia
Penguin Books Canada Ltd, 10 Alcorn Avenue, Toronto, Ontario, Canada M4V 3B2
Penguin Books India (P) Ltd, 11 Community Centre, Panchsheel Park, New Delhi – 110 017, India
Penguin Books (NZ) Ltd, Cnr Rosedale and Airborne Roads, Albany, Auckland, New Zealand
Penguin Books (South Africa) (Pty) Ltd, 5 Watkins Street, Denver Ext 4, Johannesburg 2094, South Africa

On the World Wide Web at: www.penguin.com

Penguin Books Ltd, Registered Offices: Harmondsworth, Middlesex, England

First published 2001
1 3 5 7 9 10 8 6 4 2

This story was previously published in *More Animal Stories* published by Viking 1999

Text copyright © Fox Busters Ltd, 1994
Illustrations copyright © Tim Warnes, 2001
All rights reserved

The moral right of the author and illustrator has been asserted

Set in Bembo Schoolbook

Printed in Hong Kong by Midas Printing Ltd

Except in the United States of America, this book is sold subject to the condition that it
shall not, by way of trade or otherwise, be lent, re-sold, hired out, or otherwise circulated without
the publisher's prior consent in any form of binding or cover other than that in
which it is published and without a similar condition including this condition being
imposed on the subsequent purchaser

British Library Cataloguing in Publication Data
A CIP catalogue record for this book is available from the British Library

ISBN 0–141–30994–6

Dozy was a Two-fingered Tree-sloth.

On his feet he had three toes, but on each hand only two fingers.

Snoozy was a Three-fingered Tree-
sloth. He also had three toes, but he had
three fingers on each hand.

All tree-sloths spend their lives upside down in the forests of South America. They are born upside down, they live upside down, and the only time they ever touch the ground is when they die (upside down) and fall off their perches.

Always they are facing the sky, so that they see only the tops of the trees, and when it rains, only their tummies get wet.

Dozy and Snoozy were quite different, and not just because Snoozy had more fingers.

Dozy was grumpy. He had a bad-tempered expression. He would bite, and slash with his sharp claws.

Snoozy was gentle. On his face he wore what looked like a smile. He only waved his arms about, and never bit anyone.

Dozy was brownish.

Snoozy was silvery.

Dozy was boastful.

Snoozy was modest.

Where they were alike was in the way they moved, and not just because it was upside down. It was also very, very slow.

All tree-sloths are slow, but Dozy and Snoozy were among the slowest sloths in the whole of South America.

Snoozy didn't mind this.

"Nice and easy does it," he would say gently to himself as, very, very slowly, he reached out with one three-fingered hand to pull himself forward.

Dozy did mind.

"Get a move on," he would say
grumpily to himself as, very, very
slowly, he reached out and pulled
himself forward with one two-fingered
hand.

The other creatures of the forest made fun of Dozy and Snoozy. The brightly coloured parrots screeched with laughter at the tree-sloths. And the monkeys hung by their tails right in front of the noses of Dozy and Snoozy and shouted, "Slow coach!" at them. Dozy slashed at them angrily, but Snoozy only waved his arms about, while on his face he wore what looked like a smile.

One day by chance Dozy and Snoozy met.

Snoozy was hanging under a branch having a nap when Dozy came crawling along (upside down of course and very, very slowly) underneath the same branch.

"Hey you!" said Dozy loudly. "Get out of my way."

Snoozy woke up.

"Oh sorry," he said softly, and he began to reverse. Now a sloth going backwards moves very, very, very slowly indeed, and while Dozy was waiting, he noticed Snoozy's hands.

He's got three fingers on each, he thought. Stuck-up creature. Snoozy noticed that Dozy had only two fingers on each hand. Poor chap, he thought.

"I suppose you think you're better than me?" said Dozy.

"Better?" said Snoozy. "How do you mean?"

"I suppose you think you're faster than me, because you've got extra fingers?"

"Oh no," said Snoozy. "I shouldn't think so."

"We'll see," said Dozy. "I challenge you to a race."

By now Snoozy had reversed far enough to reach another nearby branch and thus get out of Dozy's way. He didn't want to race anyone, least of all this bad-tempered sloth.

But the monkeys had been listening,
and they told the parrots, and the
parrots flew all round the forest
spreading the news.

"The Great Sloth Race!" they
screeched. "Roll up, roll up, everybody,
to see the Great Sloth Race!"

There was no way now, it seemed to
Snoozy, that he could escape having to
race Dozy.

It took a long time of course before all was ready, but at last Dozy and Snoozy were hanging upside down on two long branches that ran parallel to one another.

Then the judge, an old and wise toucan, opened his enormous beak and called, "Ready, steady, go!"

Very, very slowly, one with a two-
fingered hand, one with a three-
fingered, Dozy and Snoozy reached out
to pull themselves forward. After an
hour they had travelled about halfway
along their branches. Dozy was slightly
ahead.

Many of the animals of the forest who were watching had become bored and had flown or ran or crawled or hopped away. After two hours, Dozy was well ahead and nearing the end of his branch.

By now everyone had become fed up with so slow a race, and all had gone away except the judge.

After three hours Dozy reached the end of his branch.

Opening his enormous beak, the toucan called, "Stop! The race is over."

Snoozy stopped.

"Told you so!" shouted Dozy. "I got to the end first. I was faster than him, even though I've only got two fingers on each hand and he's got three. I've won the race!"

The old wise toucan flew down and landed beside Snoozy.

"Oh dear," he said softly. "I should have explained the rules to Dozy. I'm afraid he went too fast. The object of a sloth race is to see who can go the slower. Congratulations, Snoozy. You are the winner."

Upside down as always, Snoozy
looked up at the toucan.

On his face he wore what looked like
a smile.